THE HOUSE OF BLOCKS

Written by Cecilia Minden and Joanne Meier • Illustrated by Bob Ostrom
Created by Herbie J. Thorpe

ABOUT THE AUTHORS

Cecilia Minden, PhD, is the former director of the Language and Literacy Program at the Harvard Graduate School of Education. She is now a reading consultant for school and library publications. She earned her PhD in reading education from the University of Virginia. Cecilia and her husband, Dave Cupp, live outside Chapel Hill, North Carolina. They enjoy sharing their love of reading with their grandchildren, Chelsea and Qadir.

Joanne Meier, PhD, has worked as an elementary school teacher, university professor, and researcher. She earned her BA in early childhood education from the University of South Carolina, and her MEd and PhD in education from the University of Virginia. She currently works as a literacy consultant for schools and private organizations. Joanne lives in Virginia with her husband Eric, daughters Kella and Erin, two cats, and a gerbil.

ABOUT THE ILLUSTRATOR

Bob Ostrom has been illustrating children's books for nearly twenty years. A graduate of the New England School of Art & Design at Suffolk University, Bob has worked for such companies as Disney, Nickelodeon, and Cartoon Network. He lives in North Carolina with his wife Melissa and three children, Will, Charlie, and Mae.

ABOUT THE SERIES CREATOR

Herbie J. Thorpe had long envisioned a beginning-readers' series about a fun, energetic bear with a big imagination. Herbie is a book lover and an avid supporter of libraries and the role they play in fostering the love of reading. He consults with librarians and matches them with the perfect books for their students and patrons. He lives in Louisiana with his wife Misty and their daughter Carson.

The Child's World

Published in the United States of America by The Child's World®
1980 Lookout Drive • Mankato, MN 56003-1705
800-599-READ • www.childsworld.com

Acknowledgments
The Child's World®: Mary Berendes, Publishing Director
The Design Lab: Kathleen Petelinsek, Design
Artistic Assistant: Richard Carbajal

Library of Congress Cataloging-in-Publication Data
Minden, Cecilia.
  The house of blocks / by Cecilia Minden and Joanne Meier;
illustrated by Bob Ostrom.
     p. cm. — (Herbster readers)
  ISBN 978-1-60253-224-3 (library bound : alk. paper)
  [1. Blocks (Toys)—Fiction. 2. Hundredth Day of School—Fiction.
3. Schools—Fiction. 4. Bears—Fiction.] I. Meier, Joanne D.
II. Ostrom, Bob, ill. III. Title. IV. Series.
  PZ7.M6539Hou 2009
  [E]—dc22   2009003969

This is a rectangle. Can you find
the rectangles in this book?

Today is the 100th Day of School

It was the 100th day of school.

Herbie and Charlie were making a house.

Today is the **100**th Day of School

8

"We need to use 100 things," said Herbie.

They had lots of blocks.

First they built the walls.

Charlie put in some windows.

Herbie put on the roof.

Did they have 100 things?

Mr. Stone counted.

They had 99 things.

They needed just one more.

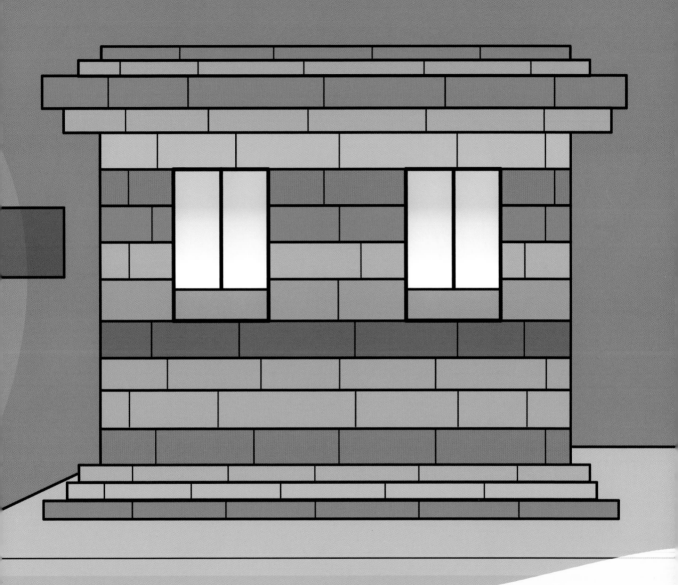

"There isn't a place left," said Herbie.

"Maybe you forgot something," said Mr. Stone.

What did they forget?

"We forgot the door!" said Herbie.

"100!" said Herbie and Charlie.